This book is dedicated to the real Maxine who I have known since 4th grade, and to the real Francie, who I have known since birth when our mothers met wheeling us in carriages in Central Park.

Also dedicated to the real Gary Igel, MD, friend and pediatric consultant on this project.

Maxine Gets Her Vaccine
Copyright © 2021 by Elena Lesser Bruun. All rights reserved. This book or parts thereof may not be reproduced in any form, stored in any retrieval system, or transmitted in any form by any means—electronic, mechanical, photocopy, recording, or otherwise—without prior written permission of the author.

Author: Elena Lesser Bruun
Illustrator: Zoe Matthiessen

ISBN | 978-1-7373847-0-0 (hardcover)
ISBN | 978-1-7373847-1-7 (paperback)
ISBN | 978-1-7373847-2-4 (ebook)

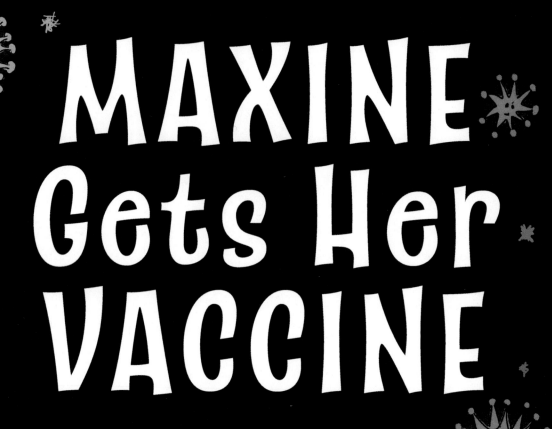

MAXINE Gets Her VACCINE

Written by
ELENA LESSER BRUUN

Illustrated by
ZOE MATTHIESSEN

It was not long ago, in the year 2020, there was a sickness that traveled far and wide called a pandemic. It took time for scientists to find a cure, so many people were afraid of getting sick and many people were afraid of the cure. This is a story of one little girl in America named Maxine who went through it all...

It's just another crazy morning at Maxine's house. Mommy and Daddy are always rushing to be somewhere, but Maxine only listens to Jakey, who clearly wants a treat.

Every night since forever, Mommy and Daddy take turns reading to Maxine.

They also read to Jakey, who seems to understand every word on the page.

Right after school, Maxine races home from school to play fetch with Jakey, who doesn't seem the slightest bit interested in the game.

Hey Jakey, no fair! They told us at the Animal Rescue place that you were a RETRIEVER! Guess not, huh?

Mommy tries to explain.
"Oh Maxine, you don't need to worry so much.
It's just a shot for dogs to keep them well."

But Maxine is still suspicious and,
according to her, Jakey is **NOT GOING
ANYWHERE.**

But of course the "discussion" isn't really over at all.

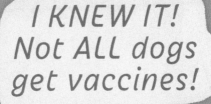

Dr. Noah explains that the shot will keep Jakey well, but Maxine is still not happy.

She presented several arguments and tried her best to convince Dr. Noah that Jakey didn't need a shot, but it didn't work as she hoped, and Jakey got his shot anyway.

Afterwards, Maxine scooped Jakey up like he was her baby. She could not wait to get him **out of there!**

Just to be sure he's ok, Maxine doesn't let Jakey out of her sight.
She spends the entire rest of the day watching him closely.

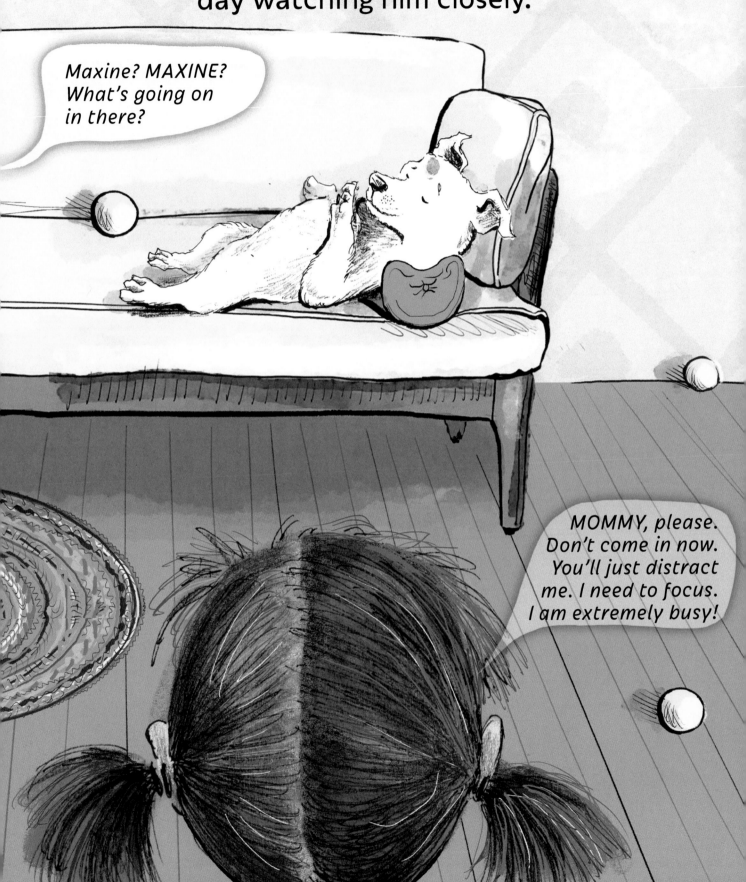

After a little rest, Jakey is back to his old self more playful than ever!

Things go back
to normal.

Jakey still
won't fetch.

Everyone
is happy again.

UNTIL...

One night, Mommy and Daddy
look **STRANGE**
when they come in to read
bed-time stories—
they are wearing masks over
their noses and mouths!

It turns out to be a very serious virus, and for days and weeks and months—even for a YEAR—everything is changed!

Mommy and Daddy are always spray-cleaning doorknobs and light switches—they spray EVERYTHING!—and washing hands takes **FOREVER!**

Maxine's favorite places close their doors, and only BORING places stay open, like grocery stores and gas stations! Even there, everyone has to wear a mask and stay six feet apart.

There aren't as many people outside, but when there are they are wearing masks in shops and on the bus, even when they ride their bikes!

Maxine and Jakey wash their
hands and paws together
a zillion times a day.

At first it was awesome when the schools had to close. Maxine and Jakey had a blast! But schooling at home is so weird and Jakey does not understand remote learning. Maxine misses her friends. She is sad and frustrated, and Jakey just wants to play!

SO EXCITED ABOUT THE NEWS,
MAXINE RACES TO THE PHONE
TO CALL FRANCIE!

It turns out Francie has already been on the phone with other kids, and she gives Maxine an earful about the new cure.

Worried, mixed up and confused, Maxine hopes her parents can straighten it all out.

Maxine's parents remind her that they got
their vaccines and feel perfectly fine—
and they promise that she will too.

Maxine is still
not sure.

That night Maxine tossed and turned and couldn't sleep.
Finally she yelled out to Mommy.

You and Daddy come here
RIGHT NOW!
I NEED YOU THIS MINUTE!

Exhausted from the
excitement and the shot,
Maxine falls asleep on the couch.

Jakey watches her like a hawk.

He wags his tail
and waits,
and waits.

Maxine finally wakes up!
She has survived the shot and feels back to her old self, alive and well.
Jakey is ecstatic!

Things go back
to normal.

Jakey still
won't fetch.

Everyone
is happy again.

THE END.

ABOUT THE AUTHOR

Elena Lesser-Bruun, EdD, LMFT (doctorate in education and licensed marriage & family therapist), has decades of professional experience. She spent twenty-five years in Medical Education, first at SUNY Downstate, and then as Clinical Associate Professor of Psychiatry and Associate Dean for Student Affairs at the NYU School of Medicine. She maintains a private psychotherapy practice in New York and virtually, seeing individuals, couples, and families.

In addition to her overall clinical expertise, she is highly qualified to speak about relationships, having co-authored several books: *Marrying Well* (Norton 2010), *Not on Speaking Terms*, (Norton, 2014) and, written during the pandemic, *Estranged* (April 2021).

Maxine Gets Her Vaccine, (June 2021) is a humorous yet important and very timely book meant to help young children lower their fear of getting their Covid-19 shots. It is Elena's first toe into the children's book world water, and she so enjoyed it, you can be sure it will not be her last.

She can be found at www.elbtherapy.com.

ABOUT THE ILLUSTRATOR

Zoe Matthiessen is a self taught artist who has received awards from The Society of Illustrators and American Illustration. She was selected by *Art New England Magazine* as one of the "Top Ten Emerging Artists of 2018" and awarded their Artist-in-Residence of 2019. She has contributed regularly to *The American Bystander* and to *The Nation*, and has recently produced an environmental children's book, *The Last Straw*, published by North Atlantic Books (Jan 2021).

View her work at www.zoematthiessen.com.

Made in the USA
Middletown, DE
22 October 2021

50767682R00022